COPPER SUNRISE

BRYAN BUCHAN

COVER BY JAMES HILL

ILLUSTRATIONS BY KATHRYN COLE

a GOLD
LEAF book

Scholastic Canada Limited
123 Newkirk Road, Richmond Hill, Ontario, Canada

Scholastic Canada Ltd.
123 Newkirk Road, Richmond Hill, Ontario, Canada L4C 3G5
Scholastic Inc.
730 Broadway, New York, NY 10003, USA
Ashton Scholastic Limited
Private Bag 1, Penrose, Auckland, New Zealand
Ashton Scholastic Pty Limited
PO Box 579, Gosford, NSW 2250, Australia
Scholastic Publications Ltd.
Clarendon Avenue, Leamington Spa, Warwickshire CV32 5PR England

Canadian Cataloguing in Publication Data

Buchan, Bryan, 1945-
  Copper sunrise

ISBN 0-590-73835-6

I. Cole, Kathryn. II. Title.

PS8553.U34C6 1991   jC813'.54   C90-095867-7
PZ7.B8Co 1991

5 4 3 2   Printed in Canada   3 4/9
Manufactured by Webcom Limited

To Anna

In one of our fields was a lark's nest, and on some days I could sit for half the afternoon watching the male bird on top of the stone wall. He liked the feel of the warm sunlight, the sound of the buzzing swarms of insects, the colour woven into the grass. It was his world, and he was in charge. I almost wanted to be that bird.

One bright afternoon I crouched in the deep grass, leaning against an old rock that had fallen long ago from the crumbling wall. The lark was sitting proudly on a bit of post that stuck above gorse bushes of the hedgerow.

His song was soothing; I began to daydream, dim images flooding my mind in rhythm with his notes, flowing and melting into one another. The real world was far away.

Slowly, almost as though it were a part of my daydream, I saw the lark stiffen. A few feathers floated out from his body as he fell from the post.

I lifted myself from the grass and moved towards the place where he had fallen. A familiar voice was speaking beside me but I paid no heed.

There, in the sharp spikes of the gorse bush, hung my lark, still alive. His bill moved slowly, open and shut. His glazed eyes stared into nothing. And again the voice at my side.

The lark's head drooped onto his twisted wing. Gradually his eyes turned dull and filmy as his life drained away. Robert was beside me, with a sling clutched in his hand.

The lark was dead—an ordinary field-bird, hanging stupidly in a gorse bush, the beautiful, magical music gone.

I turned to face my brother.
"Why did you kill him, Robert?" I pleaded.
Robert looked away from me, but I knew his face was white, and his eyes frightened.
"I didn't think I'd hit it, Jamie. I only wanted to scare it." His voice trailed away and was lost. . . .

"We are leaving now, Jamie," he said quietly.

Chapter One

During those first days at sea I enjoyed being alone. The cool sunlight of the North Atlantic in early fall made the water around the *Star of Bethlehem* glisten with thousands of happy eyes.

Behind us was Scotland and the village which had been our home. Ahead lay the unknown—new and mysterious lands waiting to be settled. After months of family discussions, Papa had finally closed up our shop and the five of us were starting on an adventure across the sea.

For hours at a time I would sit in the bow watching the waves and the images in the clouds and listening to the endless rustle of the sails. My big brother, Robert, was fascinated by the work aboard the ship and volunteered readily when extra help was wanted. My little brother, Davie, simply ran everywhere and got into all sorts of mischief. He was a great favourite with the crew and was especially fond of Mathieu, a big French-speaking sailor who spoiled him horribly. At times Davie seemed to have the whole ship under his command.

But I kept to myself. Many times Davie would race excitedly up to my post in the bow shouting and jumping. "Jamie! Come see the thick rope! Come and see Mathieu's knots!" There were many, many, such things he wanted to show me, but I was never interested. I dreamed of the new land. . .

****

It was on the sixth morning out that Davie first complained about not being able to find Mathieu. The crew began to behave strangely. They gathered in sullen clusters of two or three, muttering together. Gradually they became more excited, and arguments occasionally flared up. The groups broke up when one of us came near, and I noticed that when Davie was around, the sailors nearly fell over each other in their anxiety to avoid him. It was all very odd.

Papa soon discovered the cause of this tension. Mathieu was below decks, seriously ill. The captain was afraid that it was a plague and suspected that Mathieu had caught the disease in Glasgow. There were stories along the docks of ships returning from India with only half their crews, and that India itself was overrun with a raging epidemic. He hoped Mathieu was the only one who would get sick, but he doubted it. Only two of his crew had previously had the sickness, and the rest were in danger. The captain asked if any of our family had ever suffered from this strange and deadly illness; if not, we, too, could catch the disease. Turning back to Glasgow was out of the question since we would doubtless be refused entry to the port. It was just as well to continue.

Any feeling of seasickness became suspect, and we spent the remainder of the day listlessly watching the sea roll by. It was oppressive, and we snapped peevishly at each other.

By sunset Davie was complaining of stomach cramps. The pain grew worse, and other symptoms began to appear. He was upset by diarrhoea so suddenly that Mama had to change him and give him a bath in warmed seawater. Over the side went his trousers. After the bath, Papa lifted Davie from the tub and began to dry him. With a small groan, Davie collapsed and fell to the deck. There was fear in Papa's eyes as he carried Davie's limp body below deck and placed him in bed. Several times Davie seemed to be conscious, but he did not hear us and would not speak.

The captain had seen Davie fall. He advised us to keep away from the crew and stay in our cabin. He arranged for food and water to be brought to us. Any waste was to be thrown out the cabin porthole.

Through the night we watched Davie become weaker and weaker. He hadn't the strength to open his eyes; we feared he would stop breathing. Occasionally he broke his silence to ask faintly for water. Sweat soaked the bedding and formed a tiny puddle in the hollow of his chest. Mama had torn up some curtains to make diapers for him. Her usual soothing manner was gone. She hovered over him with anxious, frightened movements. He often needed to be changed. Many times his body was shaken by vomiting, and Mama wearily discarded the bedding and gave him fresh sheets. His skin began to shrivel, and it felt hot to the touch. When we gave him water, his mouth was dry and we could see that his tongue was the colour of milk. It seemed his heart was scarcely beating.

When morning came, our food was untouched and only a few mouthfuls of water had gone from Davie's cup. Robert and I dozed lightly in our bunks, waking up with each sound that broke the stillness.

At last Davie seemed to be sleeping peacefully. His sweating stopped, and his skin was smoother. By noon, he was eating a few bites of bread and speaking to us.

His first questions were about what had happened to him. Next he asked about Mathieu.

Chapter Two

Several more
days passed before we were allowed out of the cramped
cabin and onto the sunlit decks where we could once
again breathe deeply the sharp salt air.

Papa learned that Mathieu and two other sailors had
been buried at sea. No one told Davie where Mathieu
had gone, and he soon stopped asking about his friend.
The daily scene of wind-swept water, cloud, and sun
passed with little change, interrupted only by the cool,
clear nights of early September.

At last, after more than six weeks at sea, a thin dark
line appeared on the horizon and the captain announced
that we should prepare to land. The harbour we were

now approaching was called Cutwater. From a narrow entrance the bay thrust inland with marshes along the coast giving way to high, rocky cliffs clothed in dense forest beyond. A cluster of wooden houses perched on the rocks in a clearing at the head of the inlet. A rickety-looking jetty leaned on stilts in the calm water. Behind the houses, cod drying racks, salmon-nets, and jigging lines stretched back to the forest edge. A large black dog raced across the narrow beach to join a number of people who were stepping down the rocks to the jetty.

"I like it," said Mama, relieved to see land again and Davie excitedly agreed. Papa had spoken to the captain and while the *Star of Bethlehem* remained at anchor in the harbour, two sailors rowed us to the jetty, where the villagers crowded about us.

It was soon arranged that we should take one of the houses; the owner had been lost at sea and his wife was returning to her father. Papa paid a small rental for the winter and we began the slow task of moving our belongings into the village. The jetty was too small for the *Star of Bethlehem* so the villagers helped us unload with their dories. We landed all the supplies we had brought to set up shop in the New World together with what was left of our food.

When all the supplies had been carried to the house, Papa decided to rest, while Robert, Davie and I set out to explore the village. We were under strict orders not to

12

leave the cleared area and halted at the tangle of bushes and trees that marked the beginning of the wilderness—unknown lands that stretched for miles and miles away to the south. Underfoot was a soft carpet of dried spruce needles, cushioning and silencing our footsteps. But we did not dare to go past the forest barrier.

We had soon explored the entire village, the plank and shingle houses, the jetty, the drying rack. There were no mysteries, no secrets to excite my imagination.

But the creek was different. At the far end of the clearing it sparkled down over the rocks in a spray-making torrent that whispered, sang, shouted all at once—bringing twisted tales of strange beasts, wild people, unknown cities, all waiting upstream. To the villagers, this icy creek was just a water supply; to me, it was a magnet that pulled me to new places.

Several times during our first week in the village I tried to persuade Robert to follow the shallow creek-bed with me, just to see what lay beyond the trees, but he was always too cautious to explore. "You know about the savages, Jamie," was his usual answer.

Yes, I did know about the savages. They were the greatest reason for my desire to go upstream, and all the tales we heard from the villagers only increased my eagerness to see these shadowy beings. The fishermen and their wives spoke about strange and hideous giants who lived in the dark forests of the interior and who painted themselves red. Some people said the rock they made the paint from turned their skin red, and they could never wash it off. Other, more sinister rumours of cannibalism and murder were only half believed by the villagers. Daniel Martinson, a neighbour, told us that the savages did not dare to approach the villages, so greatly did they fear guns, and especially dogs, which they had never seen before the English arrived. He said they were a stupid, lazy race, living like animals in the woods. They were not worth worrying over, or even thinking about.

But there was little else I did think about all that rainy autumn. I longed to see one of these mysterious people, even more than I longed to see the caribou, said to be common in the interior.

Once I thought I saw smoke, and excitement mounted within me. But Robert said it was only a faint bit of mist, and it drifted rapidly away.

Winter brought new interests. A whale was beached on the shore, and we spent an entire day melting down the blubber in huge kettles over roaring open fires that made us sweat even in the chilly air. A huge white owl settled on our roof one night and remained until the following evening despite the interest we all showed in him.

Many of the villagers went out sealing in the early spring, but Papa, of course, stayed with the store he had opened in the front of our house. Sometimes, the villagers told us, the ice floes break up unexpectedly and the sealers are taken helplessly out to sea. No one was lost that year.

Icicles remained on the rocks where the creek sprayed, creating crystal bars, making recesses and hollows seem like sparkling miniature prisons. I sometimes sat and watched the snaky patterns formed by the twisting trickles as they sought the ocean. Even Robert liked the sound made by the falling ice when he snapped off the points with a stick.

Yet my brother was spending less time with me as he made friends with Andrew Watson, the only other big boy in the village. Andrew was a year younger than Robert and four years older than me.

Both Andrew and Robert were expected to help with the fishing. I was allowed to work on the drying racks, but the dories were only for stronger people. Occasionally, though, I was allowed to go squid jigging with the two older boys. But with Robert learning the skills of a fisherman from Andrew, I was left alone much of the time, with only my imagination to keep me company.

Davie had learned to leave me alone, and spent most of his time with Mama or the village dog, the only one who would listen patiently to everything he had to say.

Daniel had told us that the savages had never seen dogs—I learned over the spring that this new country also lacked a few of the commonest Scottish animals. There were no snakes or turtles, no rabbits, no squirrels, crickets, horses. A strange land, this.

By spring we had been so completely accepted by the villagers, that even Papa cautiously decided we would settle permanently in Cutwater. People in other villages along the coast would need supplies from our store and he knew how to get and sell all sorts of things: everything needed by the fishermen, food and tools, clothing and crockery, paper, glue, and nails.

Robert helped the fishermen check the dories and learned to mend the nets for the salmon runs.

Chapter Three

The warm spring weather brought a new friend to the harbour. In a deep pool below the rocks at the creek mouth, a seal had set up his home. I would sit silently beside the pool for hours at a time, watching him slip through the water, twisting and rolling in pursuit of the tiny minnows that shared the basin. He seemed never to grow tired of playing and invented games with stones, or simply chased himself up and down through the water. I was always surprised at the speeds he reached, using his flippers as the fishermen used the oars in their dories. His fur was smooth and shiny-looking, like a slippery stone from the creek-bed, and I wanted to reach out and feel it.

If I had been that seal, I would have travelled up and down the coast just to see the strange animals and mysterious savages. I could not understand why he stayed in this tiny pool when he could so easily have explored the world. Perhaps he had already seen it all; had already tried everything the coast could offer; then, tired of wandering, had chosen to settle in this peaceful pool, enjoying the small pieces of cod I often brought for him. Through my daily visits he lost almost all fear of people and would eagerly pull himself on the rocks to search for treats.

Papa had worked hard in the supply store. Soon a steady flow of people, many from distant villages, was coming in regularly for supplies. The villagers were always given the credit they needed until their boats returned from New York, Jamaica, or the Mediterranean.

It was always a grand occasion when the supply ship docked at the jetty with Papa's orders. In addition to the merchandise for the store, there were gifts for each of us. This time Davie got a small bag of sweets, the part of Scotland that he most missed. I got a copper flute, and immediately set about learning to play it. My first try at music did not meet with much success. Because Robert was grown-up, helping to support the family with his work in the dories, he got the finest gift, a rifle, something new to the villagers who, until now, had seen only muskets. He was granted permission to hunt in the forest.

The trader was invited to our house for a meal before continuing his voyage. As we ate he told us the latest news from along the coast. Most of his information concerned the savages, who had been causing great trouble almost everywhere. In many outports they had raided for iron or copper tools, even slipping past armed sentinels to steal. Sometimes they left shoddy trash, bears' tooth necklaces and the like, to mark their thefts. At Bay of Whales a whole line of hooks was stolen, and the same type of report was common throughout the villages of the north and east coasts. Here at Cutwater, nothing like that was happening, since the nearest settlement of savages was over thirty miles away, east of Port Martinson. But the trader warned us not to relax our guard, for the savages could move swiftly through the forests, appearing when and where they were least expected.

Along the east coast, people were beginning to search the forest to exterminate the thieves. Reports in town stated that almost a hundred of the creatures on the mid-east coast had been shot.

This news worried me, for I feared the savages would all be killed before I could even see one.

His meal finished, the trader belched loudly, swallowed the last gulps of tea from his mug, and rose to go on his way to Brigantine, the only other port he planned to visit. Taking my flute, I went down to see him off at the jetty, while Mama and Papa set about unpacking the merchandise they had received.

The supply ship was part-way down the harbour when the trader began to shout and wave at me. At first I only stared stupidly at him, but then turned to see a vague spiral of smoke from the hill behind the village. Savages! It could only be savages, but fearful of starting a hunt to destroy them, I said nothing and just plodded up the slope to the house.

A shot rang sharply down by the creek, momentarily freezing my muscles. An attack! But almost immediately I remembered that Robert and Andrew had gone off up the creek to hunt for game with the new rifle. I raced off to join them, my flute clutched in my hand.

Clambering over the slimy boulders near the mouth of the creek, I slipped and grazed my knee on the stones. I sat down beside the pool to staunch the flow of blood from the scrape and suddenly saw the seal—my seal—on the rock, a neat little hole in his back. His fur was still smooth and damp, his head stretched along the rock on a twisted neck. As I watched, his eyes turned dull and filmy. Rage nearly choked me, but I could make no sound and my eyes were dry. The seal was dead.

Why had Robert used the rifle? The seal had been a gentle neighbour, guilty of no crime. What had brought this punishment upon him? I had to tell Robert of his mistake—tell him that the seal had been my friend, tame, not a wild animal fit only as a target. No one had wanted him killed; alive he had been a good, playful creature.

Still bleeding at the knee, I stumbled along the rocky creek to find my brother.

20

Chapter Four

In places the creek was wide and sluggish, forming areas of marshland. I splashed through the still water, croaking Robert's name, startling the marsh birds. My breeches were wet at the knees; my eyes still burned. Each new cry I gave hurt my throat and echoed dully from the surrounding forest.

The creek again narrowed, rushing over the rocks in its downhill path. Here the balsam and spruce grew so densely that the stream seemed like the floor of a gloomy tunnel, hemmed in on both sides and roofed with green. I was forced to stumble over the stones of the creek-bed, since the thick trees on either side prevented my walking on the bank. Dead branches spiked the lower trunks, their twigs snatching and tearing at me like evil little claws. My flute slipped through my fingers into the current and I spent several moments searching frantically among the pebbles. I was relieved to discover that it still worked. Birds swirled everywhere among the tree-tops chattering at the intruder.

Robert had not answered my cries, and at last I fell silent, panting as the water flowed icily past my knees. From overhead came the harsh cry of an osprey, probably going to fish for salmon in the upper harbour. Suddenly I remembered that I was expected to gather mussels from the tidal pools for supper. But the tide would be in for several hours still.

A cracking twig in the tangle of dead branches caught my attention. On the shadowy bank was a snow goose. It was strange that he should venture this far into the trees. Cautiously I stepped along the stream-bed, hoping to keep him in sight. He continued to travel slowly upstream along the bank, stopping from time to time to peer about suspiciously, craning his neck above the undergrowth.

For almost half an hour I followed the bird along the stream, stalking so that a careless splash would not betray my presence.

At one point he hesitated, his head turning from side to side as he sought to identify something. Then he found an opening in the leaves and rapidly disappeared into the darkness. I stooped to watch him vanish.

"Ka-ah!"

The sudden, piercing cry stunned me, causing me to lose my balance. As I struggled to retain my footing, I felt terribly conspicuous and glanced quickly around me.

It was then we saw each other. Facing me, thigh-deep in the creek where it spread into a large pool, was a boy. It was his cry of triumph that I had heard, for a large fish still struggled in his hands. He was about my age, but very tall and lightly built, with straight black hair that came down over the tops of his ears. His skin was the colour of the chunk of copper he wore on a leather thong around his neck. Except for this necklace, he wore no clothing. His dark eyes stared at me, showing that he was as startled as I, and just as afraid of what might happen.

"Ni-eh?" he asked, his voice trembling, so softly I could barely hear him. I continued to gaze foolishly at him, and he repeated the question, adding several words, none of which I could understand.

My throat finally responded, doing what I wanted it to do. "Hello," I said, feeling extremely silly. Here, at last, was the savage I had longed to see. He was no doubt a cannibal, probably ready to murder me right then. But somehow I realized that he was more frightened that I was. He had no knife or weapon, and I felt sure he would not try to pursue me if I ran back to the village.

"The village!" How far away from the safety of home had I wandered? This thought made me more nervous.

Finally he spoke, nodding towards the flute I held.

"It's a flute," I said, and showed him how it was played. My short practice had not improved my skill, and the notes did not sound like any kind of music, but the boy seemed pleased. A smile spread slowly over his face, revealing white teeth with a space in front. Again he began to talk slowly in a language I could not understand, and finally held out his fish, pointing to the flute. I shook my head and he stepped back, his smile fading.

But again he brightened, showing me both the fish and his copper necklace. I suddenly realized that it might be dangerous to refuse what he wanted. I held out the flute and he splashed happily through the water to get it. He slipped the leather strap from his own neck and placed it around mine and then pushed the slimy fish into my hands, chattering rapidly. He took the flute and placed it to his lips, blowing the notes one at a time.

Gradually the notes began to flow together, blending and melting into a tune unlike any music I had ever heard before, but it seemed to carry a terrible sadness.

The boy grinned once more and poured forth a torrent of words in his strange, gentle language. Then he turned and splashed through the water to the far bank, where he pulled a strip of leather from the bushes and fastened it around his hips. Quickly he pulled a breech-cloth between his legs, and looped it over the leather strap. Without looking back, he picked up a bow and several arrows, and vanished into the trees.

Chapter Five

For a while I
stood frozen, staring vacantly at the point where he had disappeared, fascinated by this mysterious boy, so unlike the savages of the village stories.

He was no giant, murdering cannibal; I had met no sudden, horrible death. I had seen only a tall, black-haired boy, with coppery skin and a smile that showed the space between his teeth—a boy who caught big fish with his hands and played music that haunted me for hours afterward.

And he had been just as surprised, just as frightened, just as curious, as I had been. As I began wading back downstream, I decided that I liked the boy. It was almost as though a new friend had been sent to replace my seal.

The closer I came to the village, the more I began to worry about what had happened. Several times I had

been warned about the dangers in the forest and forbidden to leave the village alone. Papa could be very fierce when he was disobeyed.

And where was Robert? I knew now that he was not in the forest, since surely he could not have passed the boy I met. Then it occurred to me that he and Andrew, after killing the seal, had probably headed off down the coast to shoot stearns or other sea birds.

I edged nervously out from the trees and walked bravely down the slope with my fish.

Excited villagers were gathered on the jetty, or rowing about the harbour in dories. I was certain they were searching for me.

At the last moment I remembered the copper necklace around my neck. Hastily, I took it off and stuffed it into my pocket. My heart thumping, I gripped the fish firmly and marched down to the jetty.

Relief flowed through my muscles as I searched the dock. No one asked where I had been. Papa was out in a dory, and Mama said nothing when I came up beside her. I was safe. All this interest at the dock had nothing whatever to do with me. I had been so worried about the people that I had not noticed the water of the bay. As I now looked at it, I was startled to see that the harbour was a bright pink colour, almost as bright as the wild roses that had grown back in Perthshire. I asked what had happened.

"Jellyfish, Jamie!" cried Davie. "Pink jellyfish!

Everywhere!"

And so there were. Millions upon millions of them, stretching all over the bay, dyeing the water this strange shade. I knew they were massed deeply, since even the wake of the dories showed the same pink colour.

Where had they come from? No one knew.

Eventually people began to lose interest and the dories were beached. Mama had taken my fish and packed me off along to the tidal pools to collect mussels. Some of the jellyfish had already been washed ashore, making the rocks slimy as I worked.

Fish and mussels, a fresh loaf of bread that smelled delicious, hot tea, and much talk about the jellyfish: supper passed without anyone asking about my whereabouts during the afternoon. No one had even noticed my absence. My secret was safe.

The following day, as soon as I had finished my chores, I slipped off into the forest again, retracing my steps up the creek-bed. At last I reached the pool where I had seen the boy and paused, somehow expecting him to appear from the forest. But the creek was deserted. Wading along near the bank, I searched for the path he had taken when he left me. Strangely, I could not even find a break in the matted plants and dead branches. It was as though he had never even existed. I turned to go back to the village, sighing with disappointment, when I spotted the faint print of a bare foot in the soft soil of the bank. Although the footprint was not fresh, and the branches seemed still to be an unbroken tangle, I was now certain that the boy had at least been real. Besides, I still had his necklace in my pocket. I pressed my foot firmly into the moist ground near the print the boy had left.

Every day that week I slid unnoticed and unmissed from my family, returning hopefully to the pool, expecting him to be there. Each time, I was disappointed to find no trace of the copper-skinned boy I imagined to be my friend.

One dull afternoon, late in the week, I reached the pool to find it still silent and alone. No ripple stirred its glassy surface, but overhanging the pool, on a swaying branch, hung a fragile-looking string of beads. Cautiously I pulled them from the branch and examined them. So tiny and finely-worked were they that I thought they must have been carved from sparrows' bones. They seemed almost to glow in the overcast daylight.

I paused a moment to see if the owner of the beads were watching from some secret place, but I detected nothing. Only the distant drilling of a woodpecker broke the endless silence.

I pushed the beads carefully into my pocket, afraid that I might damage them. What could I leave in exchange? All I had was a narrow strip of red cloth which I had rescued from the refuse Papa had thrown out from the shop. I tied the bright scrap to the same branch that had held the beads, then headed back downstream.

28

Even before I reached the village I could hear Davie laughing and Mama shrieking. I edged cautiously from the forest and picked my way through the boulders by the creek. I could see Davie chasing Mama with a large lobster. Mama was not afraid of lobsters, I knew, and I chuckled at this game. Davie was really having fun.

As I came across the clearing Mama stopped, and between laughing and panting, asked if I had discovered anything interesting along the beach. I shook my head with a grin and Davie continued chasing Mama toward the house. I carefully hid the beads and copper necklace under the house, where a small ledge jutted out from a floor beam.

We met the lobster once more at the supper table, but now its blue-green shell was a brilliant red. Papa did not seem as pleased as he usually was with such a treat. Instead he stared grimly at his plate and then, with his bushy eyebrows knit almost in one angry line, looked across at Mama.

"The thieving savages raided a schooner up at Brigantine last week. Luckily most of the crew were ashore and the deck watch jumped overboard when they came. But they took a lot of hardware and two new sails from the ship.

"What would the filthy scum do with sails?" he continued, "They haven't even got a boat to rig them on. They ought to be shot."

Across the table I shivered.

Chapter Six

In the morning
Davie and I were sent with pails to catch enough crabs
for a meal. Davie was so excited at having someone to
go with that he was more nuisance than help. He managed to catch three small crabs, squealing in delight
when his prisoners threatened him with their claws.
Then he accidentally kicked over my pail, and all nine
of my crabs splashed into the water, sliding back under
rocks and vanishing. We had to begin again. Davie was at
first afraid I would be angry. When he was sure he
would not be scolded, he forgot his fear and wanted to
kick the pail once again. We finally collected almost two
dozen good-sized crabs, and clambered up over the
rocks to our house.

"That's a very fine tub of crabs you have," said Mama looking over the catch with an expert eye. "And Jamie, do you remember that big fish you brought home for supper last week?"

"Yes," I gulped.

"Why is it you've not caught another like it? Has the creek run dry, or was that one only luck?" Her eyes were laughing at me.

"Well, Mama," I began, "you don't find many that large this near the harbour. They are probably all upstream, in the forest. Shall I go catch another?"

"Now, Jamie, I don't like your being alone in those murky woods with no idea where you are. But I think if you stayed near the creek or a trail you'd be fine."

"Oh, yes, Mama," I blurted. "And farther up the stream the trees are so thick you could not get away from the water anyway."

"Now, how would you know about that, Jamie?" asked Mama. I could feel my face reddening and becoming warmer.

"Oh, away with you, you little scoundrel." she teased. "Get your fishing line and hooks and catch us another of those river fish. I doubt it will be anything as big as that first one, though."

Snatching up my tackle from the sideboard, I sped out the door to freedom. The fresh air was cool. Two village women stood nearby, watching a huge black

31

raven that was gliding over the village.

"And of that bird I don't like the sight," said one. "Them sooty vultures is a certain sign of a death approaching. It's as though there were to be carrion lying all about."

But death and carrion were far from my mind as I dashed across the clearing and into the tunnel that enclosed the creek-bed. This time my conscience was clear.

Mama could never have guessed that I was anxious, not to catch another of those large fish, but to meet again my copper friend, who could vanish into nothing and hold himself invisible.

Cautiously I approached the pool, fearing the usual disappointment, yet longing for another face-to-face encounter with the boy. I realized abruptly that I had brought nothing with me to exchange, should he have left another token. Silently I reached the edge of the pool, hoping desperately.

A light drizzle had begun to fall, misting the clearing and roughening the empty waters. It was cold on my neck, and I raised the collar of my shirt. There was no one at the pond; the vague outlines of the branches held no messages. A silver coating glowed on all the leaves, but nothing disturbed the silence.

I sat down dejectedly, feeling the dampness of the log seeping through the seat of my trousers. I knotted a hook onto my line. At least the trip need not be wasted this time.

Hardly was the line in the water when a twig snapped sharply behind me. Jerking about, I saw the boy standing with a broken stick in his hand and the copper flute thrust in his belt. The drizzle had covered his skin with the same silver gleam that the leaves displayed. A smile moved slowly across his lips and he spoke quietly, "Ni-eh?"

I grinned back. "Hello." I pulled out another hook, gave him a piece of line and motioned for him to sit beside me. A long series of soft words came forth, but none of them made any sense to me. He joined me on the long-fallen tree trunk that served as a bench. He seemed to know exactly how to use the hook and line, and chattered continually at my side.

I caught the first fish, and the boy helped me pull it in. But I really needed no help; Mama was right—it was half the size of the one I had brought home the week before. The boy pointed to the fish and said a word. He looked at me, then pointed again at the fish and repeated the sound. I imitated him, and his face lit up. I had learned my first word in the language of the savages. By the same method the boy learned his first word in English.

Then he pointed to his chest, saying his name, *"Tethani"*. I told him mine.

During that long, damp afternoon we each learned many words in the other's language. He was eager to know what everything was called, including his copper flute. His speech flowed smoothly, like the strange and beautiful music he played on the flute.

The drizzle had developed into a regular steady rainfall, and it was rapidly growing darker. Afraid of being caught in the fog that sometimes rolled in off the bay on evenings like this, and feeling less and less comfortable in my soggy clothes, I prepared to leave. I noticed that Tethani kept the hook and line I had loaned him, but I was happy to make it a gift. Between us we had taken three fish, and the two largest were going home with me.

"I will come tomorrow, Tethani," I said. "Goodbye." He repeated the goodbye in his own language, but he could not say the "J" in my name. He called me "Tamie".

I looked back over my shoulder as I groped my way along the dim tunnel towards home. He was still standing motionless at the pool with his flute. Long after I lost sight of him I could still hear his music, but how much was real and how much only memory I cannot say.

Mama was waiting anxiously in the warm house.

"Thank Heaven, Jamie, I was worried about your getting lost in the mist, lad." Then, seeing that I was all right, she smiled and added, "My, that's not a bad pair of fish you have. We'll put them in the pan for your supper."

Papa told us that fishermen from Brigantine had

called at the store. He said the savages had once again raided the town, but they were frightened off before they could steal much. They got only a cooking pot and some nails, and had dropped a bundle of trinkets including some tiny bone beads and a strip of red cloth.

"At least a cooking pot will be more use to the beasts than sails," he added. Then he peered at Davie with a grim smile: "Unless they eat one another raw."

Chapter Seven

During the whole time that Robert and I spent jigging for squid the following morning, I continued to wonder about Tethani. That piece of red cloth found at Brigantine after the raid: was it the same piece that I had given to him? I could not force myself to believe that my friend would have been guilty of the crimes the savages committed along the coast. He was different from the rest.

And yet, Brigantine was not far away. Only a day's travel, or less, on foot along the twisting shoreline.

Robert had hooked another squid and was pulling it carefully over the side of the rowboat. He laid the squirming creature on the floor and removed his hook. Neither of us liked the taste of squid, nor the feel of their soft bodies, but they were interesting enough with their ten thin arms, like strands of seaweed, and their stumpy, rounded bodies, tapering off into fluke-like tails. In the water they moved by shooting backwards in short jerks, reminding me of stones skipping over the water. I was even half-convinced they could change colour, although no one ever said so.

Robert had been telling me about some of the adventures he and Andrew had had as they explored up and down the rocky coastline. Once they had spotted whales bobbing and slapping the water with their broad tails. They had also taken the rowboat across to the islands off the point, where sea birds by the thousands laid their eggs. Andrew had been in a vile temper all the while, fuming and complaining and in general ruining the egg gathering with his black mood. The highlight of the trip had come when he stomped back to the boat and plunked himself down on the thwart with a scowl. His scowl turned to shock and then to rage as he discovered that he had sat down on his cap—which contained all the eggs he had collected. He had leapt to his feet, almost overturning the boat, the day's work running in yellow and white streams down his trousers. Andrew had been so furious that Robert had not even dared to smile, but now he almost collapsed with laughter. Panting and gasping, he gave a startling imitation of Andrew's whining voice.

Then his face clouded abruptly and, very serious, he leaned towards me.

"Jamie," he hissed. "Can you keep a secret if I tell you? No one else must ever know but I can't keep it inside me any more."

I was astonished. Since the incident of the seal, Robert and I had not been on the best of terms. I was always uneasy, even a little frightened, when I was with him.

"If I told Andrew," Robert continued, "he would just report me to his father, and I'd be kept at home if Papa found out about it. But you wouldn't betray me, would you Jamie? You're only a little boy, but you're a good lad, eh?"

My mouth must have hung open, but somehow I managed to nod my head. How strange that my grown-up, dependable brother should have a secret he wanted to keep from everyone except me, his little brother. I wondered what it was that he had done wrong.

"We were down the coast a few days ago," he began, "Andrew and I. I had my new rifle with me because we were looking for geese in the tidal marshes beyond the point. We were moving very carefully so that the birds would not hear us. As we were creeping along by the bushes I saw something that scared the breath out of me." He paused, his hand tightly gripping the jigging line, his face pale.

I could not take my eyes off his. "What did you see?" I gasped. I had never seen Robert like this.

"Andrew didn't notice, thank God," Robert continued. "He always watches the sea, like a true fisher-man, I suppose. But I was watching the forest, Jamie, and that's where they were. I didn't know what to do. I could scarcely move my feet, I was so frightened."

"What was it?" I pleaded, almost off the seat with

excitement and curiosity. Robert was becoming even more tense, and I was afraid he would begin to cry.

"It was a woman, Jamie, one of the savages. I supposed later she had come out of the forest onto the shore to collect crabs or mussels or something. There was a little boy with her. They were partly hidden in some bushes above the rocks."

The boy! I thought quickly. Had Robert shot them? I slid forward off the seat, soaking my knees in the water that covered the rowboat's planking. I forced out the words, "What did you do, Robert?"

Robert was reliving the event. His face was white and twisted.

"Nothing," he replied. "That boy was just a little child, younger than Davie. How could I shoot them? It would have been like putting a bullet through Mama and Davie. But they were savages. Was I wrong to let them go, Jamie? Did I make a mistake?"

I closed my eyes, blinking to get rid of the tears. My muscles loosened and I breathed deeply. Without speaking, I leaned forward and hugged Robert's knees. The boy he had seen was not Tethani, and he had killed no one.

"What's wrong Jamie? Why are you crying?"

"I'm not crying, Robert. I was afraid you had killed those people. I'm just happy you didn't."

Now Robert also relaxed, and I could hear his breath coming in gulps above me. The hard muscles of his thigh began to unwind from their tight bands, and I released his knees. When I was back on my seat, I glanced at Robert's face. He was smiling now, but his eyes were still running.

"I'm glad I told you, Jamie," he said. "Don't give me away, please don't."

My face must have reassured him. As we rowed back to the beach, he described the woman. She was surprisingly tall, with reddish-brown skin. Strings of white beads were wound through her long black hair and bound across her forehead. The same beaded threads were looped into a necklace and bracelets. A sleeveless dress fell from her shoulders. It seemed to be made of grey skin, probably caribou. He could not tell how long the dress was because her legs were hidden behind the bushes.

The boy stood beside her, partly hidden by the same bushes. They were perfectly still, and seemed very frightened. Robert had glanced away for a second to look at Andrew, and when he turned back, the woman and boy were gone without a sound.

"I thought perhaps they might bring someone to kill us," he went on. "So I dragged Andrew home. I told him I felt sick, but I don't think he believed me. He sulked all the rest of the day, complaining about his spoiled hunting."

Robert and I reached the shore in silence and climbed onto the beach.

40

Chapter Eight

Despite the chill rain which began falling, as usual, in the early afternoon, I set off happily to find Tethani. The quiet at the pool was disturbed only by the steady dripping of the rain; I sat down on the log to wait. The ripples on the surface made flowing patterns, circles expanding outward to melt into other circles, blending in a constantly changing tracery of motion. Time crawled by, bringing no break in the rain and no sign of my friend.

Soon I began to wonder if he had understood my pledge to return this afternoon. After all, he knew only a small handful of English words; "tomorrow" would mean nothing to him.

And then beside me I heard my name mispronounced softly, "Tamie", and Tethani came through the bushes, his bare shoulders beaded with glistening raindrops, his black hair soaked and lying flat against his head. In one hand he held his bow and several copper-tipped arrows, in the other a piece of iron, ground down to a fine knife-like edge. The flute stuck out over his leather belt. He was smiling widely; his teeth and eyes glinted even in the dull misty light, laughing like the summer stars. The space between his teeth made his grin seem still broader.

He pressed the iron blade into my hand, and showed me how to use it for scraping. It may have been made to clean skins, carve wood, scale fish. It was difficult for me to understand anything he said, but we communicated fluently with smiles and our own signs and signals.

At length he stood up, motioning me to follow him into the dense bushes. For a moment I hesitated, thinking of what Mama had told me about the forest. Tethani grabbed my wrist and tugged me after him. "You must never go alone," Mama had said. I was not alone; I need feel no guilt.

He seemed to know his way among the tightly inter-woven trees, finding openings in the matted bushes, walking through thick brush as if it were only a lace-work of fern. The branches scratched at me, tearing my face like thorns, but Tethani seemed hardly to touch them.

Several times during the journey he stopped to point out animal tracks. His very serious imitations of the animals were designed to explain whether the tracks had been made by caribou, moose, or fox; but I enjoyed the pantomime for its own sake.

Gradually I became aware that the knotted thicket of branches and dead trees on our left had not grown there. Many of the trees had been cut down and dragged together to build this dense wall, which was much higher than my head. It was clearly a very old wall, covered with vines and other plants, but its outlines were still recognizable. I wondered what the wall was for, and pointed it out to Tethani, asking him what it was.

He stopped and began an explanation in his own language. I recognized only the words for "hunt" and "caribou". He pantomimed both the caribou and the hunter, making the situation even more confusing; but I assumed that this long barrier had been woven to hide or protect the hunters when they shot their arrows at the caribou.

Satisfied that my question had been answered, Tethani continued along his invisible trail.

When we had come about a mile from the creek, we were abruptly faced with a solid wall of rock, a thick shelf that ran off to left and right for many yards, and rose straight up for about twelve feet. The ground in front of this cliff was clear but several dead trees stood along the rock itself.

I now noticed another of the caribou barriers angling in through the forest to touch the cliff face, about twenty feet to the right of the first. Tethani was climbing up a tree and balancing along a straight limb to reach the cliff-top, beckoning to me to follow him.

From the cliff-top the pattern made by the fences became clear. It was as though we stood at the point of a huge letter "V", whose arms could be seen wherever the trees were thin. Tethani drew the "V" on the soft soil with a stick and poked several dots about, telling me that they were caribou. As he drew in more details, the whole plan became obvious.

The caribou were driven down between the two fences, which gradually came closer together and made a narrow pathway. When the animals reached the little clearing below us, they were trapped by the fences between the cliff and the hunters who had chased them. Sometimes more hunters would be waiting on the cliff-top, but there were seldom enough men both to chase and to wait above. Sometimes, Tethani said, there were many caribou; often the people nearly starved.

We continued along the trail until suddenly Tethani stopped and stooped down without warning. Taken by surprise, I tripped over him and fell headlong into the bushes. My hand was black from a piece of charred wood I had brushed against and I turned to Tethani in alarm. What was wrong?

Tethani laughed and showed me the reason for his abrupt stop. All around us in this small, burned-out clearing were blueberry bushes, sprouting from among the blackened rocks and stumps. Tethani's tongue was

44

already stained with purple, and I lost little time in joining him, gorging myself with fistfuls of the tiny, tangy-sweet fruit.

The rain had stopped without our noticing it and a rare burst of sunlight flooded the berry-patch with gold, making the beads of moisture glisten on the leaves.

At last we rose and Tethani led on through the forest. Here the ground began to rise. Rock showed more often through the earth floor, and the trees grew less densely, until at length only a few rotting stumps could be seen, surrounded by a thick growth of chest-high bushes.

At the summit of the hill we reached a cleared area, with a fire-pit and a scattering of charred bones and bits of antler. I felt that this place had lain unused for a long time.

Tethani pointed far to the north. The bright sunshine, which glistened on the damp green of the forest, showed us the broad expanse of the bay, and the narrow inlet jutting in to Cutwater. The village clustered like grey pebbles on the shore. Off in the distance Brigantine could be seen. I breathed in the cool breeze that flowed off the sea.

Tethani smiled his open grin again and turned me about. Below, on the opposite side of the hill, were two cone-shaped huts made of branches and bark, covered with canvas.

I began to wonder if I had been wise to follow Tethani this far.

Chapter Nine

Tethani was already scrambling cheerfully down the hill towards the camp. I felt only panic as he went; my heart was pounding and my throat dry. Yet I had very little choice. If I followed Tethani to the huts, I might be murdered by the cannibal giants the villagers had described. If I turned to run, there was little hope of finding my way home through the vast forest. I would wander endlessly among the dense growth until starvation or a bear ended my suffering.

In the end, it depended entirely on Tethani. If he were truly my friend, there would be no danger below in the huts. But if he had betrayed my trust, the trap had already closed, and escape was impossible. I followed him down the hillside with throbbing head.

Tethani called softly before we reached the camp, and a woman's voice replied. Turning to me he began to search through my pockets and pulled forth the sharpened iron fragment, the scraper that he had given me when we met at the pond. He put it in my hand. I was so nervous that I thought it was for self-defence, and I stayed close beside him as we entered the sheltered clearing in front of the huts.

A tall, slender woman was kneeling on the ground beside the cold ashes of the fire-pit scraping at a deer skin with a bone cleaning tool, hollowed out and moulded at one end to provide a sharp lip. Pushing the tool across the hide, she glanced up nervously from her work and spoke softly to Tethani. Her words were quick and fearful. Tethani smiled and replied in a calm voice that eased the strain in her face. He said my name, and she repeated it, making the "J" a "T", just as Tethani did.

From her appearance, I guessed that this was the same woman Robert had seen when he had been hunting geese. She had skin like Tethani's, and long black hair ornamented with strings of the delicate sparrow-bone beads. Her grey dress fell to below her knees, and she wore leather slippers that appeared to be sewn from a single piece of skin. I supposed she was his mother, although she looked very young.

A small boy, a little younger than Davie, stumbled sleepily from a hut, rubbing his eyes. When at last he had them opened far enough to see me, he gave a sharp cry of fear and ran to fling his arms about his mother. She soothed him with soft words and stroked his hair until it was smooth. At last he peered cautiously over her shoulder at me, and I smiled. Tethani spoke gently, urging him over.

He was taller than Davie but lightly-built, like Tethani, and had the same copper-coloured skin. The leather strap around his hips and the breech-cloth it held were made of the same softened grey hide. Around his neck was a thong to which was fastened a bone whistle.

Tethani picked him up, and the boy hugged him tightly, as if he were afraid of being put down again. His eyes continued to search me.

Tethani nodded towards the child. *"Shadothai"*, he said. Then he pointed at me and spoke to the boy, "Tamie." We had been introduced.

The worst part of my visit began when Tethani let his brother slip smoothly to the ground and signalled me to follow him into one of the pointed huts. Earlier I had noticed that a rough metallic scraping sound was being made in one of these huts, but it was so low-pitched that I had forgotten about it. Now again I heard the rasping of metal on stone, and my fears returned. I had visions of the cannibal giants sharpening their blades for the slaughter.

Tethani pulled me into the hut through the low doorway. A faint patch of light from this entrance was the only relief from the gloomy darkness that blotted everything from my sight. There was a strange smell in the hut, not unpleasant, but stale; the odour of smoked meat and soot mingled with it to give an impression of decay and disuse. The floor was damp and cold, probably just packed earth.

While my eyes adjusted to the darkness, Tethani began speaking in his soft voice, and again he said my name. I was startled to hear a man's voice say my name in a tone much harsher and louder than Tethani's. By now I could see someone dressed like Tethani and Shadothai sitting in the dim shadows of the room. Near him was a pile of arrows and a large copper cooking pot, with many pieces cut out of its rim. Several arrows had copper tips, probably fashioned from the missing pieces of the pot. A rough stone lay in front of him for sharpening them.

In the centre of the hut was a cold fire-pit, and around the walls were pits dug into the earth, filled with branches to make beds. A few furs and caribou hides made up the bedding. Overhead were racks hung with a few fish and several pieces of meat ready to be smoked when the fire was lit. Bones littered the ground, but they were caribou bones, not human.

"Tamie!" grunted the man again. Tethani pushed me forward, motioning desperately for me to give the man the iron scraper I still clutched in my hand. After staring stupidly at the blade for a few painful moments, I offered it to him. He snatched it from me and grunted a few rough words, very different from the way Tethani and his mother had spoken. And yet this man must be Tethani's father.

He grunted again, and Tethani led me from the hut.

I stood blinking in the brilliant sunshine of the late afternoon until Shadothai shyly approached and offered me a piece of cold roast meat. I recognized the word for "caribou", and repeated it with a smile. Shadothai chuckled happily and ran to the cover of his mother leaving me to chew on the smoky meat. As Tethani and I ate, I examined the campsite carefully.

The two huts were like blunt cones, covered with what I knew was sail canvas. I now knew at least what savages, who had no boats to rig sail on, would do with sailcloth.

About the site were scattered many articles and tools, looking as though they belonged there and had been there for a long time. This campsite was not new.

There were roughly worked stone axe-blades and the heads of stone adzes, finely chipped flint points for bird arrows, and baskets and containers made from bark sewn with plant roots. I picked up one of the flint points, admiring it as I turned it over and over in my hand. I had never seen flint in this country and I asked Tethani where the stone had come from. He only shrugged and pointed vaguely to the south, towards the interior.

Shadothai had slipped the bone whistle from his neck and was playing a low note. He pulled the copper flute from Tethani's belt and handed it to his brother. Tethani played his same drifting music which seemed to me both beautiful and sorrowful, then sadly put the flute back in its place.

Pointing to the reddened sky, Tethani warned me that the sun was dangerously near the horizon and we had to begin the hike back to the coast before it grew dark.

I heard Tethani's father singing a strange song in a deep and mysterious voice, completely different from the grunting I had heard earlier.

We stood to go.

Chapter Ten

The sun had sunk low in the sky
by the time we reached the silent pool, and the forest
had become a vague mist of unfamiliar shapes. I wondered how Tethani would be able to find his way home
over the dim trails, trails I could not follow even in
daylight. Night would bring an inky covering to everything in the woods.

But Tethani's cheerful farewell gave no hint of hesita-
tion or fear. He slipped mysteriously away through the
trees and left me alone in the still twilight.

I picked my way carefully along the gurgling creek-
bed, slipping on the smooth stones, clutching at the
branches in the darkness. I began to wonder if anyone
had missed me.

They had. Long before I reached the village I could
hear shouts echoing through the night and see the flash

of lanterns at the end of the narrow tunnel I was following. I shouted in answer and the lanterns clustered at the tunnel's mouth ahead of me.

This was the first time I had stayed away after sundown. Mama and Papa were long used to my absences; ever since I could walk I had gone off whenever possible on my own. But now I had overstayed the time limits. I started to arrange lies in my mind to explain my late return.

"Jamie! Thank Heaven you're safe!" cried Mama, hugging me into her warm arms. The darkness had been cold.

"Where were you, lad? What have you been doing?" demanded Papa sternly. "Did you not know we'd be worried about you?"

I told them I was sorry for upsetting them and said I must have fallen asleep while I was fishing. I did not even have my fishing lines with me, but no one noticed, and my lie was accepted as an excuse.

As we went back to the house, Robert laid his arm across my shoulder and walked beside me in silence. The candle in his lantern had gone out. I knew why he had been worried over my disappearance.

I had expected to be thrashed severely with the ladle, but got only great numbers of hugs from Mama and Davie. Robert signalled me to keep quiet. I somehow managed to eat the cold fish they had saved for me. It was stale and greasy, and the clammy chunks felt horrible in my mouth, but I swallowed them quickly and washed them away with tea. I much preferred the roast caribou that Shadothai had given me.

When Robert and I were in bed, and he was certain Davie was asleep, he began to explain what had happened that afternoon. He had been afraid, he said, that the savages had killed me and was blaming himself for not shooting the woman he had seen at the shore. If he had not been such a coward, he felt, they might have been frightened off and I would have been safe.

I learned, also, that today had been a bad day to stay away after dark. Fishermen from Cape-of-Islands had called in to Cutwater and during their visit had reported that there were vague rumours of savages migrating along the coast in large numbers. They usually lived in small groups, the fishermen said; the large bands meant that food was becoming scarce. To Mama, there seemed only one food they would be interested in.

The savages were raiding more often along the north coast, and more and more things were being stolen: sails, shovels, axes, pots, fishhooks, nails, ropes, gaffs and harpoons. At Port Martinson they had killed a dog and carried it off with them. So far, no deaths were reported in the north, but they had heard that several dozen savages had been shot down on the east coast.

Robert knew that the savages lived in the forest, making it unsafe even by day, and nightfall only increased the risk. Night was when the savages made their raids. What if they found me?

I told Robert that I had never seen anything dangerous in the forest and he seemed somewhat relieved. But several times during the night I was awakened by his troubled tossing and groaning. In the dim light I could see beads of sweat on his forehead, and the pillow was soaked.

During breakfast Papa continued his stern lecture. Like everyone else, he had feared that I had been captured or killed by the savages and carried off to their camp.

I thought once more of Tethani's camp and frowned, remembering how discourteous and unfriendly his father had seemed. Why had he not been more polite?

"You know, Jamie, that if you stumbled on those wretched creatures in the forest," added Papa, "there would be very little hope for you. I don't know what they'd do to you, lad, but if one of their boys wandered in here, I'd grab Rob's rifle and blow his head open. What then would a savage do to you?"

I repeated my story that nothing dangerous had ever crossed my path; I had seen fox prints once, but they had been old and faint.

The matter lost its importance, and little more was said. I expected Papa to order me never to go again into the forest. Perhaps his warning was meant to forbid my trips, but I worked around it in my mind.

That very afternoon I again met Tethani. We stayed

at the pool to fish, he with his hands and I with my hook. He seemed to enjoy splashing about, plunging into the cold stream to grab a fish, letting it go if it was not big enough for him. Somehow he always seemed to catch the largest fish, but I managed to pull in two good ones. They would make a welcome meal.

I was rapidly learning his language and could understand much of what he said. He, too, seemed to know a greater amount of English and could follow my meaning even when I spoke of my home which he had seen only from the top of the sighting-hill.

He was especially interested in hearing about Davie, for he had never seen anyone with yellow hair. He even asked me to bring Davie with me to the pool so that he could see him, but I had to refuse. My parents would have been horrified if they had known, and Davie could never have kept quiet about the trip if I tried to bring him secretly.

Tethani was afraid to come near the village, so Davie and his light hair remained a strange mystery for him.

I knew, though, that Shadothai was certainly no mystery for Tethani; he was half his life. He spoke proudly of the little boy, boasting of how Shadothai could already shoot a bow accurately enough to hit the mark, but lacked strength to reach a bird or animal. Although Shadothai's arrows often fell uselessly to the ground, Tethani felt sure the boy was destined to become a great hunter. There would be no fear of starvation when Shadothai began to hunt.

Tethani sang me a song of his people, describing a hunter's search for moose. He acted the roles of both the eager hunter, whose family would starve if he failed, and the stately figure of the moose, whose death meant life for others. He played the parts so well that I was sorry when the song ended.

Then he took out his copper flute and Shadothai's bone whistle. While he played the flute I sounded the mournful note of the whistle and the two blended into music more remote and ghostly than even he alone could produce.

Long before the sun even threatened to set, I left Tethani at the pool and returned home, making sure to come up to the house from the beach as though I had been away exploring the rocks. I watched from our small window as the sky clouded over and fog rolled in off the grey surface of the bay, and wondered about my friend in the forest.

Chapter Eleven

The next weeks were unusually warm, and Tethani and I spent hours together, basking in the welcome sunlight, throwing pebbles at a rock or climbing to the sighting-hill, which Tethani's people used to follow the movements of the caribou. We fished in the creek or swam in the fresh water of the pool; we played hide and seek among the clumps of bushes; and often we just talked. I memorized the trails and became almost as familiar with the forest as Tethani. I learned many things from my friend and taught him about life in the village.

Once, after we had left his camp, I asked why his family had built the second hut. I knew they all slept together in one room and that the other hut lay empty all the time.

Tethani said nothing but led me through the forest to a part of the hill which I had never seen before.

Here an overhanging ledge sheltered a row of wide cracks in the rocks, and earth had filtered down to form what looked like a series of roomy cupboard-spaces, shallow caves with mossy floors. One of the openings had been blocked off with a heavy rock, and plants had begun to seal it from view.

Tethani sat down on the carpet of needles that covered the forest floor and ran his hand gently across the stone that closed the first cave. He turned to me with solemn eyes. His face remained without expression while he told me about his grandfather and grandmother. They had lived in the second hut, sharing it with a younger sister of his father.

A great sickness had killed his aunt, his sister, and both his grandparents, covering their bodies with tiny sores that left their skin pitted and rough. The marks could still be seen when the bodies had been washed and prepared for burial, coloured with red ochre and ornamented with beads and fine caribou skin robes. All four had been laid in this cave and the rock placed over the entrance, sealing them in their darkness.

"Were you very sad when they died, Tethani?" I asked. "I mean, did you cry?"

Yes, he had cried. He explained that his people believed that death released the spirit of a person, freeing it to begin the long journey to the pleasant land in the West where it could be happy forever. He had put his sister's bone flute in the cave with her body, so she would have it in the Western Land. She had played it well, and he had loved to hear the notes rising and falling like the waves of the sea, or a bird sailing the unseen currents of the sky.

She had been gentle; she had looked after Shadothai while his mother worked; she never complained. It had been hard to lose her. She would be happy now, free from her sickness in the New Land, but he still missed her greatly. During the time of illness, he was afraid that Shadothai, too, might be taken from him. He would always be grateful that his little brother had lived to share his life.

He paused, and I thought of Davie. How close he had come to death during our voyage. I began to wonder what it would be like if he had died of his sickness, and found myself suddenly grateful that he had lived. The feeling was new to me: I was glad he hadn't died, of course, but this sensation was deeper and stronger. I knew how Tethani felt.

I asked Tethani how they knew when the spirit of a person reached the New Land in the West. Did they ever return to their families?

Tethani showed me the copper flute, fingering its smoothly polished surface. It glowed in the shade as he cradled it in his palm. Copper was a beautiful colour, he said, the most beautiful of all.

When his sister had died, he explained, they waited for the messages. Every morning the family rose before dawn, walking to the sighting-hill to watch the sunrise. After a new spirit reached the West, it would send two messengers. One was the sun, who journeyed daily to the land of the West to shine on the souls who lived there, then returned to this land each morning to tell of new spirits in the Pleasant Country. The sun would rise from the eastern sea and shine brightly across clouds and water, bathing the world in copper-coloured light, softening the land and comforting those left behind. Only when a new spirit was safely at rest did the sun have that copper glow.

The second messenger always came right before or after the sun rose, appearing as a bird, or sea animal. When the sun had dawned to tell of the arrival of his sister, aunt, and grandparents in the West, the family had been greeted by an eagle that swooped low over the hilltop. They were glad that the spirits would be content. But Tethani longed to hear his sister play her flute once again. There was sorrow in his eyes as he looked at me, and he blinked to erase the tears. I stood and looked away, but he understood my thoughts, and rose beside me.

He said that someone always came to fill the empty place of the person who left, just as I had appeared after his sister's death. He had only to await the sun's message.

Together we walked slowly back to the hilltop, stopping to gather a few wild berries along the trail. Although the sun was still high overhead in the afternoon sky, Tethani slipped away from me quietly and left me to find my way home. While I slid down the moss-covered side of the hill, I heard the far-off notes of Tethani's flute, and I felt my eyes once more begin to fill.

When I reached the village, I noticed Davie sitting by himself on a rock, stroking the black fur of the village dog. I walked over and picked up my little brother who seemed to weigh less now than I remembered. He eagerly threw his arms around my neck. He must be lonely, I thought, with no one except the dog to share his world.

"Let's go for a boat ride, Davie," I suggested. "Go tell Mama where you'll be." He raced off over the rocks in great excitement, the dog yelping and barking happily at his heels. I fetched the oars and bailed several buckets of stagnant, greenish water from the boat. Even the row-boat seemed to be lonely, isolated and neglected among the larger dories on the beach.

Over the slope towards me came Davie, leaping and bouncing, his face bright with smiles. He could go.

We rowed slowly across the harbour to the tidal marshes around the point. Every time a duck or sea-bird flapped awkwardly from the water with loud cries of alarm, Davie would shriek with laughter. He chattered in his shrill voice, delighted that someone would listen, fascinated by the things he saw all around him.

A group of seals played water games at the harbour mouth, bobbing and diving, lunging and escaping in their own kind of tag. Davie could not take his eyes off them, and wanted to stay forever, but suppertime was approaching. I rowed around with one oar and then headed the boat in towards the village.

We pulled the rowboat up over the pebbles of the beach, above the high-tide level where the waves could not reach it. Then we climbed the bank to the house, Davie clinging tightly to my hand, skipping along and humming to himself. At the door he stopped to face me.

"Jamie," he said, "I like it when you take me with you. Can we go again?"

I nodded and smiled, and Davie smiled back. His teeth were loosened at the front, and there was a space between them.

Chapter Twelve

The tiny rocky islands off the coast were always covered with thousands of sea-birds. In the spring the villagers went there to gather eggs, making the short trip across the bay in dories. When Tethani asked if I would go with him to catch sea-birds on the island, I agreed readily, without even thinking of the problems we would have to face.

To begin with, even the two of us together could never handle a dory in the open bay. The oars for the rowboat were usually kept in someone's house. Sometimes there was even heavy traffic from the fishing grounds, or along the coast. What if we were seen?

But Tethani had no intention of being seen; the expedition was to be made at night, before the moon was high. All I needed to do was meet him at the pool; he would arrange everything else. Foolishly I gave my promise to come, wondering how I could ever get away to wander through the forest at night.

So, of course, I did not ask permission. My whole family usually went to bed soon after sunset. Before long the house was dark, and cautiously I rose and dressed. I searched with my bare feet along the rough wooden floor boards to find my shoes, and quietly pulled them on. I was afraid to make the faintest rustle, since Robert slept lightly, often waking in terror if a door slammed in the distance, or if someone dropped a boot.

Stealthily I unlatched the door and eased out, gently closing it behind me. The cool night air chilled my face and body, making small bumps march over my skin. On the clothes rope was a heavier shirt of mine, but it was still wet, and I left it hanging. I slipped silently away from the steps and across the clearing to the stream.

There I paused, peering uneasily into the blackness. What if Tethani had not come? He could be ill, or lost, or confined at home. I hated to enter this gloomy cavern where bears, or worse, might even now be waiting. Nervously I edged into the forest, expecting some snarling beast or horrible cry to greet me. But I had to keep my promise.

The woods were unexpectedly peaceful, and even the creek noises were hushed and muffled by the inky night. I followed the trail almost from memory, hesitating at points to listen to the sounds of the water as it gurgled over lips in the stream bed, making tiny laughing cataracts. I knew all the waterfalls on the creek, and their cheerful presence kept me company, reassuring me in the darkness.

Tethani was already standing at the pool and immediately led me off down an unfamiliar trail. After a few words of greeting, he fell silent, and we followed the path without speaking for half a mile.

There was no moon, but ahead I could make out the edge of the forest, and the unusually still waters of the bay beyond. Tethani suddenly stepped into a dense thicket of bushes and asked me to help.

Carefully hidden among the branches, so that no one walking along the beach would even notice, was a canoe. We pulled it out and carried it to the water. I was surprised at how little the craft weighed and how fragile it looked. I had never seen a canoe before—each side was shaped like a flattened crescent moon. The little vessel was made of bark, sewn with roots over a wooden frame, waterproofed with spruce or balsam resin.

Tethani held it steady while I entered, stepping carefully on the wooden ribs. He pushed it off as he swung himself into place, and handed me a carved wooden paddle.

I had never before used a paddle and I was at a loss how to handle it. Tethani said nothing but I managed to learn how to hold it by watching him slice smoothly into the cool salt water.

The islands were bunched like grapes a short distance from the point. We paddled swiftly along the coast and across the narrow strait, coming up along the side of the island that was safely hidden from the village. Across the harbour mouth, on the shore closest to Brigantine, were the salt marshes that Davie and I had visited a short time before.

Tethani backed the canoe in and we lifted it ashore between two large rocks which jutted out of the sand.

I left my paddle in the canoe, but Tethani brought his with him as we stepped across the bare rocks to a higher ledge. In a few minutes we had climbed the rough slopes to the top of the narrow rocky cliffs where thousands of gannets, puffins, auks, cormorants, and gulls were squatting in sleep. The whole island seemed to be covered with these birds, just as were all the islands along the coast. Some, like this, were home to different species; others held only one kind.

Tethani was on his knees, speaking gently to the birds. He explained that his family had no meat, that his father had gone south to hunt for caribou or moose and his mother and brother were very hungry. He asked their pardon for disturbing them at night, but he could not come during daylight.

Then he stood up, gripped the paddle tightly, and brought it down on a large gannet. He clubbed two more birds and turned to me.

"That is all we will need," he said. "We can go now."

I was glad to leave, for the moon had begun to rise in the cloudless sky, shining so brightly that I could see my shadow. I was afraid that late travellers coming along the coast might spot our canoe and open fire on us. They would certainly not stop to ask whether we were both savages before they started shooting.

Tethani picked the birds up by their feet and I carried the paddle as we headed back towards the canoe.

The bay lay calm below the cliff, and the rocks were smooth and damp with dew. There between the two large boulders lay Tethani's canoe. As we approached, my foot struck something in the darkness. I felt myself falling forward. . . .

Chapter Thirteen

My next awareness was of a dull, throbbing pain in my head, and a sharp aching in my left arm. Suddenly I was afraid to open my eyes, and yet even more terrified of keeping them closed. I looked up, and then painfully turned my neck to one side. It was all very confusing. Where was I lying? What had happened? My mind withdrew once more into the black comfort of unconsciousness.

I woke again and managed to look about me. I was in Papa's bed at home with a pillow beneath my head and the covers pulled lightly over my shoulders. Davie was carefully smoothing a cool, moist cloth over my forehead. When I opened my eyes, he gave a shrill squeal of joy, and my skull was pierced by the sound. Mama hurried up to silence him and she told me to stay calm and not to worry. Again I fell asleep.

At last I was able to keep myself conscious and I asked what had happened. The explanation left me more confused than I had been when I first awoke.

During the night, Mama said, she heard the dog barking. She listened carefully, for she had heard that savages were moving down from the direction of Brigantine. Suddenly she heard my cry from the doorway followed by a loud banging on the steps. She screamed at Papa and rushed to the door, flinging it open without thinking that outside might be a savage ready to shoot. But there had been no danger. Instead there was I, crumpled on the rocks beside the steps, my face bloody and my eyes shut. Mama thought I was dead until Papa checked my breathing. With Robert's help they carried me gently into the house and got me into bed, wiping away the blood and dirt from my head and face.

All the following morning Davie had been in charge of my comfort, washing my forehead, constantly rearranging the blankets. I had been moved to Papa's bed, so that Mama could keep a closer watch on me, but Davie had taken it upon himself to look after me.

The wounds on my head were not serious and did not require bandages. My arm hurt the worst, but no one could have known about the pulled muscles while I was unconscious.

I fell asleep from time to time during the day. Davie often came to talk to me and see if I needed anything. Mama began stuffing me with bits of my favourite foods, and I drank tea until I could no longer face it. I was still unable to remember what had happened the night before, although I was beginning to recall the trip to the island with Tethani.

The events made even less sense when Robert came in from fishing in the bay. He asked how I felt, then, making sure we were alone, suddenly leaned low over me and whispered, "What really happened last night, Jamie?"

In a frightened voice I asked what he meant.

"You know what I mean," he replied grimly. "Mama and Papa think you were walking in your sleep when you fell off the steps, but I helped get you back to bed, and there are things that just don't make any sense."

"What things?" My voice shook as I asked the question.

"A lot of things." He stared hard at me, as if he expected me to speak. "Look, Jamie, I was awake when the dog started barking last night. I didn't know you were gone, because Davie was beside me. But I do know one thing: the voice that cried out at the door wasn't yours. If you had fallen on the rocks next to the porch, the way they say you did, you'd never have made that banging sound we heard on the steps. Those scrapes on your head, Jamie—they weren't fresh; the blood was matted and dried in your hair. And there were bloody feathers on your clothes. I looked this morning, and there were no bloodstains on the rocks by the door. You didn't hit your head there. And the strangest part, Jamie: when we carried you in everyone was too excited to notice, but while I undressed you for bed, I felt your feet and legs. Your shoes and the ends of your trousers were soaking wet. The dew wasn't that heavy on the steps, lad. Now you tell me how all that fits together, Jamie boy. This isn't just another of my nightmares; this time it's real, I know it."

"I don't know, Robert. I can't remember what happened last night." I groaned and began to cry.

"Don't cry, Jamie," Robert pleaded. "I didn't mean to upset you. I only wanted to know."

I did as he told me but only because each time I tried to clear my nostrils a sharp pain shot through my head. I said nothing, and looked at the ceiling.

"Maybe I could help you, Jamie. I can keep secrets too, you know," Robert said simply. He then walked away and left me to think about the strange parts of this puzzle. Nothing made sense.

Several days later, when I had recovered enough to begin my usual wanderings, the riddle was solved.

Following the trail to the sighting-hill, I soon discovered Tethani gathering partridge berries in a rocky clearing. When he saw me he shouted happily, dropping his basket and scattering the bright red berries everywhere among the rocky crevices. From his happy chatter I pieced together the events of the "sleepwalking episode".

As we were climbing down the cliff towards the canoe that night, I had suddenly slipped on the damp rocks and thudded in a small heap on the beach some ten feet below. Tethani immediately dropped the birds he was carrying and scrambled down the ledges to my side, afraid that I was dead.

Relieved that I was at least breathing, he dragged me to the canoe and laid me out in the bottom. He then returned to the foot of the cliff to collect the paddle and the birds.

The moon had risen quite high overhead, colouring everything with a pale hazy light as he rounded the point. The village stood clearly in its glow as he paddled the canoe, with me still unconscious in the bottom, across the harbour toward the jetty. Silently he beached the canoe and began to drag my limp and heavy body ashore. My feet splashed noisily into the shallow water, and for a few agonizing moments he feared the sound had woken someone. With difficulty Tethani hauled me up the rugged slope; then he paused in panic trying to recall which house was mine. Although I had pointed it out to him many times from the top of the sighting-hill, the village looked completely different from where he now stood.

With relief he noticed my shirt pinned to the clothes-rope, and dragged me to the house. He hoped that no one was awake to see him, and laid me carefully on the rocks by the steps. The dog must have caught his scent for he began to bark furiously. Tethani's heart pounded wildly; he clenched his fists, swallowed hard, and yelled as loudly as he could, kicking at the porch to awaken my family. Then he raced away to hide beneath the jetty, terrified that the dog would break its rope and rush to attack him.

From his hiding place he watched anxiously while I was taken into the house; then, when the noise and excitement had died down, he stole back to the canoe and slipped silently from the harbour.

I realized the courage that the trip had needed. And what would Mama have thought if she had known a savage was watching them carry me into the house?

A wide grin brightened Tethani's face. "I am glad you are well again," he said. "Now you can help me gather berries."

Chapter Fourteen

The warm weather came
to an abrupt end and the days were troubled by rain or
by fog. The woods were deserted: almost all the birds
had left for the warm south. It seemed as though the
cold autumn was taking its revenge, angered by the
delay in the departure of summer.

I spent my time roaming the damp, misty forest with
Tethani or playing about the village with Davie. Robert,
like the skies, had become very gloomy and he seldom
spoke to anyone. Not even his friend, Andrew, could
cheer him up. Mama began to worry that some sickness
had come upon him and spoke about it in low, anxious
whispers to Papa.

76

A fisherman at Port Martinson had been killed during a raid by the savages, shot by another villager in the confusion. There was talk all along the coast of an expedition to punish the criminals who had indirectly caused his death, but people were too afraid to venture into the woods. Nothing was done.

One morning we awoke to a day even more dreary and damp than the many dull days we'd already had. A drizzling rain and a heavy overcast promised no relief from utter boredom. I decided that I would spend the morning entertaining Davie.

My little brother could scarcely wait to finish breakfast and start playing soldiers. I wrapped my coat around my shoulders and made my way down the slippery bank to the beach, where I could collect a basket of smooth pebbles. Each pebble was a soldier in our play armies, and thus we could have as many men as we needed.

I fastened my coat more warmly as I scooped up the stones. A strong wind off the bay was blowing icy spray onto the rocks, and the crashing waves threatened several times to soak me.

The basket filled, I turned with relief toward the warmth of the house, grabbing at the small tufts of dead grass as I pulled myself up the bank. There by the porch, fallen from the secret ledge where I had hidden it, lay the copper necklace Tethani had given me. Beside it, casting greedy eyes on the piece of shiny copper, was a huge black raven.

I ran towards the bird, afraid it would fly off with the necklace. Pebbles scattered in all directions from my wildly swinging basket. The raven refused to move as I approached. It edged even closer to the copper fragment. Then, with a harsh croak, it flapped its wings and swooped away only to land on a post by the jetty, leaving me to snatch up the necklace and stuff it into my pocket. I sighed with relief and returned to collect the pebbles I had lost.

The raven remained perched on the jetty post, looking like a seagull that had flown up the chimney, and croaked hideously.

Only then did I notice the tall schooner anchored out in the bay and the cutter that crept shoreward across the rough waters. It held a passenger.

The appearance of the unfamiliar ship puzzled me. Our trader was not due for another week, and no one else ever came to the village. I watched until the boat had reached the jetty, where the raven flapped frantically, croaking and screaming in great excitement, never leaving his post.

The helmsman steadied the cutter, his shoulders hunched against the cold rain, while a heavy, balding man, dressed in fancy town clothes and a rain-cape, heaved himself onto the dock and began to march up the slope. I watched until he beat sharply on Andrew Watson's door with his stick and then disappeared inside.

I was soaked by the time I reached my own house and reported the stranger's arrival to Mama. Then I set up the pebble armies with Davie. Soon the fat man was far from my thoughts.

A heavy pounding on the door brought a sharp cry of fright from Mama. It was Andrew Watson, asking Papa if we could come right away to a village meeting at his house. It was very urgent and important, said Andrew.

Papa agreed, and soon we were all trudging through the rain to the Watsons'. The house was almost full. Everyone in the village was there, talking of the foul weather and wondering why we were all summoned to appear.

The Watsons' table had been moved to one end of the room, and Andrew's father sat importantly behind it. At his side, looking very dignified and stern, sat the fat man. He puffed heavily, his red nose and cheeks glowing as if they were sunburned. His tiny eyes glanced suspiciously around at everyone in the room. He was waiting to speak, but as yet, no one was listening.

At last he cleared his throat violently and called for silence. He inhaled with a noisy wheeze and began to speak.

"Friends! Let me introduce myself, I am George Wilfred Craven. I have come to speak to you about the safety and security, the sacred defence, if you like, of this, our North Coast. You know well, my friends, how our glorious armies, our heroic fighting men, have time and again thrown down the tyranny of France in Europe; how we have so successfully held back the rebels in His Majesty's southern colonies. It therefore seems more strange—more strange I say—that when all these snivelling foreigners tremble at the might and glory of the King of England, here on the North Coast we should be subject to petty raiding by a handful, a very few, unwashed, mindless vermin.

"But that is not the worst of it. Only last week, my friends, these heathen savages, these barbarous murdering wretches, had the gall and effrontery to slaughter, in cold blood, a subject of the King, a fisherman who resided peacefully in your neighbouring village of Port Martinson."

His little eyes glanced quickly about the room.

"When I heard of this ultimate piece of cowardly treason, my friends, I wept. Yes, I wept, that the noble stock and race of Britain should be thus horribly outraged by these cut-throat infidels."

He looked as though he might begin again to weep.

"It was then, my friends, that I and many of my associates decided it would be necessary to rid the land of these foul animals, who prey on the blood of innocent villagers like yourselves. To that end, I have raised my own private militia and have been promised the co-operation of fishermen along the coast in this heroic and historic struggle against the evil forces of the savage. I come to you now, asking your help in wiping this hateful menace from the face of the earth. I trust, my friends, that I can rely upon your complete co-operation?"

Throughout the crowd there were murmurs and questions. Finally someone spoke.

"What is it you want from us, sir? In Cutwater here, we've had no trouble with the savages. I doubt if there are any along this part of the coast."

Mr. Craven looked at him with a sneer, then spoke to the crowd. "My friend," he stated, "the heathen are everywhere. They strike suddenly and without mercy. We must strike first. Watson, here, tells me you have seven muskets in this settlement. We will need all of them for the hunt."

Chapter Fifteen

We plodded silently home
in the dreary rain, leaving Mr. Craven to set about organizing his headquarters in the Watsons' house. He would inform us later of his plans.

I was sick with anxiety about Tethani and his family, and tried desperately to convince myself that they would easily escape the hunters.

That night Mr. Craven unfolded his plans to the villagers. Candles spluttered miserably on the table, casting insane shadows across the walls and ceiling. He did not know that an enemy spy was in his campaign room. I listened carefully to his strategy, hoping I would be able to warn Tethani.

His ideas were complex. He knew that the savages were beginning to raid the coast for food. The hunting must be bad, he said, the savages near starvation. That was exactly as he wished, for he would feed them.

Meat was to be hung from trees in the nearby woods, where the savages would be able to find it. The trees were to be hung also with the metal tools and fragments that the savages were so fond of.

Both meat and tools, he chuckled, would be prepared with a special seasoning which he had brought with him. It was made from powdered arsenic, the deadliest poison he could find.

"I hope the brutes enjoy their meal," he laughed. "It will be their last."

He gave orders for snares to be made from fine wire and strung over any trails the savages were known to use. He explained that the savages were very tall, taller than the fishermen, so the snares must be set above the men's heads.

Some of his militia would begin to comb the forest, aided by fishermen from Port Martinson and Brigantine. He would take another group of his men with those from Cutwater, and seal off the south in case the savages should head for the interior. It was vital that not one escape.

When he learned that two of our seven muskets were so clogged with dirt and rust that they could not be fired, he flew into a rage. His red face became even more intensely scarlet, and he sputtered and fumed like the candles. He accused the owners of the muskets of disloyalty, and warned us all in a stern speech of the danger of neglect and laziness. He ordered the remaining firearms brought forward. Papa sent Robert to get his rifle.

With the weapons stacked before his table, Mr. Craven announced his battle plan. Robert was to go with five other villagers and the militia to seal off the south. Andrew Watson, who had no gun, was granted permission to go along to help swell their numbers. The hunters would leave Brigantine and Port Martinson at dawn three days later. The following day Mr. Craven would lead the Cutwater men inland to block off all escape. The savages were to be flushed from hiding and shot on sight.

I glanced at Robert and was frightened to see how pale and sick he looked. He said nothing, and I did not dare to speak.

Mr. Craven gave instructions for the snares and bait to be set out the following morning. There were no questions. After a short speech of encouragement, he dismissed us to our homes.

That night my sleep was troubled by wild and horrible dreams of death and loneliness and despair. I was running away from something; it kept coming closer and closer, croaking and screaming; I was too terrified to turn to see what chased me, and I always woke up before I was caught. The pillow was damp.

Twice the whole family was roused by terrible screams from Robert. Even Davie was in tears, although he did not know why.

I slipped away at dawn and climbed the hill to find Tethani and his family. I explained quickly what was being planned and pleaded with them to run for the safety of the south before muskets blocked the way and it might be too late.

But they would not leave. There was too little game in the south. If they left the coast, with its supply of fish, they might starve. They would risk the dangers. I do not think they really understood what was happening.

Tethani and I decided to follow the party of men who would set out the snares and poisoned meat, undoing their work as we went along. His father stayed in camp to protect the others.

When we reached the hilltop, we saw the schooner sailing smoothly away towards Brigantine, probably taking Mr. Craven to complete the plans for the hunt. Tethani smiled, but I felt a tightness in my stomach.

In very little time we came down the hill and neared the edge of the village. We could hear the men discussing where best to lay the snares. Andrew's shrill voice poured advice everywhere. I knew that Tethani was terrified at the sight of so many villagers, and I admired his calm appearance as we lay on our stomachs on the damp, prickly carpet of needles.

At last the nervous group of villagers set off into the woods, fearful of their own noises, expecting death or capture at every turn. I knew that if Tethani or I had roared at them, they would have run for their lives. But we had more important work to do that day.

As the chunks of deadly meat were hung in the trees and the bits of metal looped on the branches, Tethani and I watched closely from the bushes. The trees looked pretty with their sparkling decorations, decorations which would kill anyone who used them.

The moment we felt the men were safely out of hearing we took the long poles we had cut and gingerly poked the meat and ornaments from the trees. The copper and iron made a happy tinkling sound as it fell; the meat landed with a heavy thud. We scraped enough earth with our hands and with sticks to bury the whole poisoned assortment.

The men were generous with their deadly gifts, and we had to use our poles many times. We found deadfall snares strung across faint trails, and tripped them with the poles. We were always afraid that the slashing of the snare through the branches and the violent crash as it hit the ground would alert the men to our presence.

At one point, Tethani had snapped his pole and was searching for another in the bushes while I cautiously tripped a snare. Suddenly Andrew Watson stepped out of the trees.

"Jamie, you poisonous little brat," he roared. "If that's your idea of a prank, it's a bloody poor one. Get home before I hand you over as a traitor!"

Andrew stooped to pick up the knife he had come back to get, and walked off angrily towards the others.

When Tethani emerged from the bushes, he was paler than I had ever seen him and his dark eyes stared wildly.

I thought I was going to faint.

Chapter Sixteen

Tethani and I were seldom
separated during the next two days, but our hearts were
as overcast as the grey sky. We hardly spoke to each
other and much of the time Tethani played the copper
flute. Two late flights of ducks passed over, heading
south. Several times we saw ravens.

Andrew had not reported my tripping of the snare,
and I had ceased to worry about him.

On the second leaden afternoon, Tethani and I sat on
top of the wind-swept sighting-hill, watching the campsite. He played his strange haunting music, interrupting
it frequently to tell me of some little experience he had
shared with Shadothai. By now I realized how deeply he
felt about his little brother. The thought that Shadothai

might be hurt in the hunt worried him much more than anything else. He longed to protect the boy, but did not know how. I tried to reassure him, but somehow the words would not come to my lips. I thought of Davie, and wondered how I would feel if it were my brother who was threatened.

At last Tethani stood up and turned to me, his eyes filling.

"It is almost over, Tamie." He left me and walked down the hillside to his home.

I watched him sadly until he reached his camp and disappeared into the hut, then I, too, rose to go home. In the bay far below was Mr. Craven's schooner, and several boatloads of men were rowing slowly across the harbour to Cutwater.

I felt myself panicking: running, trotting, sliding and falling down the trail in my anxiety to reach the village. By the time I arrived, the boats had docked and Mr. Craven was barking commands to his men as they set up camp in the damp clearing by the salmon nets.

We all fell asleep that night to the music of the strangers singing at their campfires. I had no dreams.

Long before dawn I rose and dressed. As I bent forward to lace my shoes, I was startled by a hand on my elbow. Robert's tense voice came through the darkness. "Good luck, Jamie," he said.

Gingerly I pushed the door open and felt the cold, damp air on my face. I eased out and crept past the sleeping men and dozing sentries. I could smell the ashes of their fires, but no smoke was visible.

Wet leaves stroked my face as I plunged into the dark forest and raced along the trail to the pool. I felt my way from there through the dim shadows, desperately trying to reach the sighting-hill.

The sun rose behind a thick wall of cloud as I gained the summit, where Tethani and Shadothai soon joined me. Below, in the village, we could see columns of smoke rising from the morning campfires, and similar columns rose from the forest in two lines, one between the hill and Port Martinson, the other towards Brigantine.

We sent Shadothai back and slipped down the hillside to the creek in time to hear the last of the men pass, coughing nervously. For a long while we sat quietly by the pool, watching the ripples expand and die. We stood and turned back to the hill.

We had barely reached the caribou run when we heard crashing noises in the bushes, thudding footbeats and cries of alarm and pursuit. Gunshots rang out, and I pulled Tethani into the tangled caribou fence, overgrown with vines and evergreen shrubs. We huddled together under the fence, hidden by the thick needles.

Almost immediately we saw people running. Tall people, lightly built like Tethani, one of them leading a little girl by the hand as she ran through the trees. They were strangers, but dressed like Tethani's family. Close behind came two men, firing, then pausing to reload. Tethani's fingers tore into my arm, and sweat dotted his forehead.

"Shadothai," he whimpered.

When I was certain the pursuers were well away from us, I crept out from my hiding place. I made Tethani promise to stay there, hoping to find his family and bring word back to him.

I pushed my way up the trail to the sighting-hill, but I knew already that it was too late. All across the hillside bushes had been broken and bent, and blackened powder wads told the rest.

From the top of the hill I could see a pattern in the chase. The position of the hunters was marked by the tiny grey puffs of smoke that rose when they fired their muskets. The lines from Brigantine and Port Martinson had joined up with men from our village to form a wide half-circle that was gradually tightening to enclose Cutwater, the rocky points along the coast, and many of Tethani's people. How many I did not know.

But now I turned to the camp. I could see from the hilltop that it had been discovered; the cloth was torn from the roofs and the side of one hut had been knocked in. There was no sound, no movement as I fearfully went down the path. I dreaded to enter the camp, unsure of what I might find.

The ashes of the firepit showed a heavy foot-print that had scattered dead charcoal. The tools Tethani's family used were lying about as usual, but a bark basket of dried berries had been trampled into the soft earth. Spread across the campsite were the strings of fine beads that Tethani's mother usually wore.

I was shaking as I approached the hut. The canvas from the roof hung over the doorway, and I raised it with a sick feeling in my stomach. The same stale smell of old fish, old soot, old leather filled my nostrils.

My eyes adjusted to the darkness and I saw that the hut was empty.

Chapter Seventeen

I paused only long enough to search frantically among the trees around the camp, then ran madly down the hillside towards the creek. Several times I caught my foot in twisted roots and slid headlong through the dead leaves and twigs on the forest floor. I felt bruised and aching, but I had to find Shadothai and his parents. There was still time left to save them.

The gunshots rang louder now, and more often. The hunters were beginning to close ranks as the circle tightened. I skirted the edge of the noisy ring, looking for an opening. I even thought briefly of taking the rowboat along the coast and rescuing them from the opposite side, ferrying them to the safety of the islands. But there was no longer enough time.

At last I reached a part of the circle where the woods were silent. I had found an opening in the trap and headed towards its centre.

But I was stopped sharply by a shot fired immediately ahead of me, and I cried out in fear.

"Who's that?" called Andrew's voice from the bushes.

It was several moments before I could speak. "Me, Jamie!"

"Get over here, you stupid fool, before the savages kill you!" Andrew pushed through the bushes and grabbed me by the wrist, dragging me back to his post. He was not alone.

Robert and Mr. Craven were advancing through the woods with their weapons held ready. My brother had the same sick look I had seen earlier, but Craven was shouting with excitement, urging his party forward with cries of encouragement. I hated him.

The four of us ploughed through the shrubbery. Craven fired occasionally; he and Andrew shouted without stop. Robert and I followed in silence.

All at once we pushed through a thick clump of trees and found three people. The man was obviously hurt; his leg was twisted and he groaned in pain. The woman and little boy were trying hard to bear him up, but he was too great a burden.

I recognized Tethani's family at once, just as our spluttering leader raised his weapon. Robert was lifting his gun beside me.

"No!" I screamed. But two shots rang out, and Tethani's mother and father lay still in the undergrowth. Shadothai was crying loudly, trying to lift his father from the ground.

"Blasted musket! The lock is jammed!" yelled Craven.

"There's another, Robert!" shrieked Andrew. "Fire again, before he escapes!"

But Robert was leaning against a tree, vomiting wildly.

"Give it me, then!" Andrew grabbed the rifle before I could even think. I flung myself at him as he fired. The explosion left me stunned, but in my daze I could see that Shadothai, too, was dead. Robert was on the ground.

Andrew turned on me. "That's twice you've got in the way, you filthy brat!" he hissed, and brought the butt down on my skull.

I reeled around, determined not to lose consciousness. The world was twisting violently out of balance, but I kept my awareness. Andrew and his companion had gone ahead.

Robert was conscious again and groaning. I pulled myself up.

"Come on!" I said. "We've got to find them."

We staggered on through the woods toward the crackling of muskets. Twice Robert fainted and I had to bring him around. The blood from my torn scalp oozed through my hair, making warm trickles down my forehead and into my eyes. I had scraped my arms, and the dirt and needles from the forest floor still clung to me.

At last we were again behind the hunters, easing slowly through the forest to the coast. The trees gradually thinned out and rock showed grey underfoot. The sea smell in the air warned me that the bay was near.

And then the hunters burst from the forest cover and halted on the open rock.

Grouped tightly on a narrow point that jutted severely out into the bay were about eighty of Tethani's people: mothers, fathers, children, young babies and old men stood facing us with solemn eyes. Behind them was a sheer drop of about sixty feet. They waited.

The hunters hesitated a moment, uncertain what to do next. But Craven knew.

"Fire!" he yelled.

Chapter Eighteen

I half-guided, half-carried Robert back home. Mama was shocked by our appearance, and anxious to get us washed and into bed. She sat Robert down and took my hand. Her hair was smooth, her dress clean, but I could sense the pain and fear in her heart.

"Now, let's wash you off and then you can rest," she soothed. "I hope the savage that hurt you has been punished."

"Let me go!" I shouted, tearing from her grasp and through the door. I had to find Tethani!

But Tethani was gone when I reached the caribou run, and I scrambled up the trail to the campsite. It, too, was deserted.

I was dazed by his disappearance, and feared he had been discovered and killed. I hurried back down the hill, heading for the place in the forest where his family had been shot. It was dusk when I reached their bodies, and more rain had begun to fall, making a steady rhythm as it dripped from the trees.

Tethani was there. I stood silently watching him as he knelt beside Shadothai's body. At his side was a bark container, filled with water. He used a small bunch of crumpled fern as a sponge to wipe the blood from Shadothai's face. He moved his hand gently across the boy's eyes, as if he expected them to open.

I spoke his name and he turned to face me in the twilight.

"Tethani," I repeated, "I'm sorry." My control faltered and I began to cry. Tethani said nothing until I became still again, then he asked simply, "Will you help me, Tamie?"

Without words we finished washing away the blood, and the fresh, cold rain made the bodies glisten even in the half-darkness.

"We must take them home, Tamie." He lifted Shadothai carefully, like a sleeping baby, and we set off through the forest towards the campsite.

It was a long journey among the dark trees and we stumbled many times. We took turns carrying the small burden until we reached the sighting-hill. Tethani carried his little brother down into the hut, and I spread the sailcloth over the floor for Shadothai to lie on.

We set out to make our second silent journey, carrying with us the other sail. As we crossed the creek we saw lanterns flashing among the trees, and heard people calling my name, but we easily avoided them in the night.

When we found the bodies again, we cut poles and made a litter from the sail. We placed Tethani's mother on the canvas and walked slowly and painfully back along the same trail, avoiding the branches and roots.

At the creek, all was still and the lanterns were gone from the forest. Only the steady splashing of the rain falling through the leaves disturbed the peaceful blackness.

We laid her beside Shadothai and made the third trip for Tethani's father.

As we finished this task, the grey light of morning was beginning to filter softly through the thick clouds, slipping among the trees to seek its own secret places.

The rain had ended, and a faint breath of air was moving through the forest.

Tethani picked up a digging tool and walked slowly along the hillside to the clearing where we had gathered partridge berries. In places the soil lay deep between the rocks, and he dug bit by bit until he uncovered reddish earth. We had forgotten to bring a basket, so I carried the earth in the front of my shirt.

When we returned to the camp, Tethani pulled the branches away from a storage pit and took out a container of seal oil. Into the oil he mixed the red earth, stirring it carefully. The red liquid became smooth and lustrous as he worked.

We used it to anoint the bodies of his family, colouring them the way his people were always coloured before burial. We wrapped them in pieces of the canvas and carried them down the hillside to the row of caves.

One beside the other we placed them in the shallow opening, Shadothai's small body between his parents. Tethani could not bear to see Shadothai alone, so we lifted him over near his mother, where he would have comfort.

Tethani returned to the campsite to get the gifts their spirits would need for the journey to the West; he brought them sadly to the cave.

He had a delicately carved whale bone breastplate for his father, and several copper and iron blades. Over his mother he laid a hooded cloak made from soft grey caribou skin, beautifully decorated with fragile, sparrow-bone beads. The hood spread over her shrouded head like a halo and the lines of tiny beads seemed almost to glow faintly in the cave's pale light. Beside her he laid the tools she used every day; she would need them in the West.

For Shadothai he brought the bone whistle and the tiny bow and arrows his brother had used. He laid them beside the child, and his hand rested briefly on the little body.

I felt in my pocket and found the copper necklace Tethani had given me so long ago. I placed it on Shadothai's chest and said goodbye. By the cave-mouth Tethani laid the gifts of food and water for the journey and together we struggled to roll a large boulder across the opening.

Tethani looked at me and smiled. "They will be happy in their new home," he whispered. Tears were entering his eyes for the first time since I had met him, trickling over his lashes and staining his cheeks. "Tamie, I'm all alone."

And that was how I left him, alone by the grave. As I walked wearily back to the village I could hear the mourning notes of the copper flute, rising and falling in a magic song of death and the long spirit journey to the West—crying for those left behind.

The village was still and lifeless. Silently I eased my way through the unlatched door of our house. I could hear my mother sobbing, speaking in short gasps to Papa.

"What is happening to us?" she pleaded. "Why are these things going on? Jamie has disappeared, Robert's mind has left him. Even Davie refuses to eat or smile. In God's name, what is wrong here?"

I tried to step forward, to reach her and tell her I was home, safe. But I felt myself falling into darkness.

Chapter Nineteen

When I awoke

I began to learn what had been happening during my absence. After I had burst out the door, Davie had sat staring out the window without speaking. Refusing to eat supper, he had fallen asleep still at the window and was carried to bed. As soon as he was awake he had gone back to the window and stayed there until I came home.

They were also terribly frightened about Robert. He just stayed in the chair where Mama had put him after we returned from the hunt. He did not speak or move and seemed not to hear. His eyes were open, but he saw nothing through them. His mind was gone.

I found myself between the smooth, stiff sheets of Papa's bed. I had slept all the previous day and night, without waking for even a minute. Mama was glad to let me rest, and my breathing had been deep and regular. Davie, convinced I was safe, had begun to eat enthusiastically, making up for all the meals he had missed. He became a guard at my bedside, and plagued Mama every few minutes with new demands.

And now he was still underfoot, risking scalding as Mama poured boiling water into the tub, helping her stir in the cold water until the bath was ready. While I bathed and washed away the caked blood and the dirt of the hunt and the burial, he never stopped asking questions. Where had I been? What had happened? Was I frightened? Were there bears? Why had I stayed away all night? Was it cold in the woods? I thought he would never be quiet.

I answered vaguely, leaving him dissatisfied. He twisted up his face and wiggled his loose teeth, accusing me of teasing him. But he kept on, and his questions flowed rapidly all through breakfast until at last Mama took him away.

I crept carefully through to see Robert and found him in bed, staring at the ceiling with unblinking eyes. There was no expression on his face, but his chest moved faintly up and down.

"Robert," I whispered. "Robert, are you all right? It's Jamie. Can you hear me, Robert? It's Jamie."

His eyes stared blankly at the ceiling. He did not answer.

I repeated his name, and touched his arm, but he seemed not to hear.

I was rising to go when I noticed a tiny movement in

his eyes. I began to talk to him, not daring to pause or hesitate. Soon his eyelids began to blink, and he tried to focus on my face.

"Jamie," he moaned, and closed his eyes.

I pleaded with him to get better, to smile, to talk. He opened his eyes and gazed steadily at me.

"Jamie," he said. "I killed her. How can I change that?" His eyes returned to their unseeing stare.

I could hear Papa in the next room, speaking angrily with Mama and left Robert to see why.

He had been to the Watsons' and was expecting Andrew's father at the door any time. Andrew had met my father and told him that Robert and I had been in league with the savages. We had betrayed the whole village, he said, and the family was being punished for our treason. He would not give back Robert's gun.

Papa had slapped him across the mouth and told him to keep the rifle.

Andrew's father did not come.

That day my family watched me very closely, and it was not until the following morning that I could slip out to see Tethani.

I found him still kneeling beside the grave. He looked tired and ill, and I knew he had not eaten since I left him. He smiled faintly when I spoke, but his dark eyes were dull and far off.

I knelt beside him, and he spoke without turning his head.

"Something has gone wrong, Tamie," he said. "Each morning, before dawn, I climb to the hilltop, waiting for the copper sunrise and the messenger from the West. But there has been no messenger, and the sun hides himself behind the clouds. Their spirits have not made the journey; something keeps them here. What is it, Tamie? Did we not leave enough food? Did we forget something they needed for their journey?"

I did not know. I told him of how I had been home and unable to come back sooner. I explained about Robert and the strange sickness he had.

"What has happened cannot be changed," Tethani said simply. "My people are dead; your brother lives. He must not torment himself because of his part in their deaths. He must live and find peace. You can heal him, Tamie."

I nodded, and begged Tethani to come home with me and eat. He would not come to the village, but he agreed to wait by the cliff-end of the caribou run until I returned with food for him.

I ran home and began filling a small basket with fish, bread, and some raisins. I told Mama I had a friend who was very hungry and she made no attempt to stop me or to keep me in the house. Out of the village I fled, along the trail to the caribou run.

I arrived breathless in the little clearing. At the edge of the cliff sat Tethani, playing the copper flute. When I approached, his eyes were shining. Some secret happiness had filled them, a happiness I could only guess at. He looked better than I had seen him for a very long time.

I looked up at him through the dead tree. "I brought some food," I said.

"That is good," he replied. "It will be needed now."

"Tamie?" He paused. "I know now what more my people need for their spirit journey to the Western Land." He rose slowly to his feet, his eyes focussed on the trees behind me.

"What more, Tethani?" I asked.

His answer never came. A shot rang out behind me, and I saw Tethani's body slip off the cliff edge and catch sharply in the tangled branches of the dead tree. His arms were held straight out from his sides; his feet and legs hung limply.

Beside me was Andrew, a smoking musket in his hands.

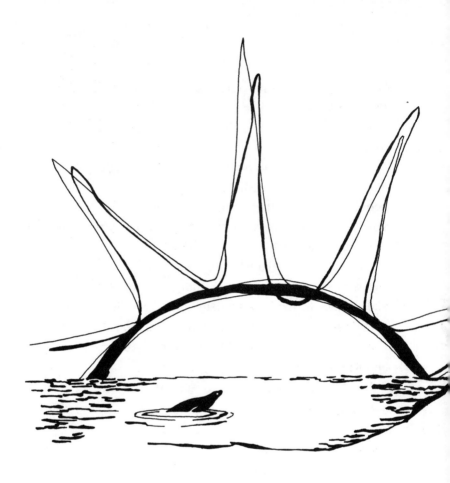

Chapter Twenty

Tethani was supported by the leafless tree, his arms still extended, and a smile on his lips. Trickles of blood ran from a wound in his side. His head had fallen forward against a branch, and the sharp twigs stuck into his forehead.

I dropped my basket and ran to help him down, but I knew it was too late; Tethani was dead. Gently I eased his light body from the tree and laid him in the soft moss. Taking off my shirt, I stooped to moisten it in a small pool of clear rainwater and began to wipe the blood from his brown skin.

He was taller than me, but he did not seem heavy as I carried him up the sighting-hill to his home. I found more seal oil and collected the red earth to mix the burial colour. Another piece of the sail had to be cut off. He was anointed and then wrapped in the rough canvas.

I walked down the hillside to the grave with my still burden. How would I ever roll away the boulder from the cave mouth? It had taken both of us, using all our strength, to move it into place.

But the rock moved easily in my hands.

I laid Tethani's body in the space between his father and Shadothai then went back for gifts to put into the grave with him.

I gathered up the basket of food I had brought. In my pocket was a knife; the copper flute still lay at the top of the cliff.

I returned again to the cave and laid the gifts beside his still form. It was not hard to roll the stone back across the mouth of the grave. I leaned against the cold rock and cried a long while for my friend.

I walked back shirtless in the cold afternoon to the village. I had expected a scolding and a beating but got instead a kiss and a new shirt. Davie sat beside me on the bed to show how loose his front teeth had become.

All that long afternoon and evening my family were very quiet. Even Papa would place a hand gently on my shoulder. It was almost as though they knew what had happened.

What had Tethani meant this afternoon? What was the one more thing his family had needed for their journey? If only I knew, I could maybe help. Why was he smiling when he fell? Had he seen Andrew in the trees? The questions tormented me through the rest of the day.

And I remembered also what Tethani had said about Robert. I told Robert that nothing was his fault but he would not believe me. He asked if Tethani had forgiven him. I explained quietly about the lands of the West and how the messenger and the copper sunrise told of the spirits' arrival.

But he asked if the copper sunrise had been seen, and I had to admit that the dawn had been clouded every morning.

"Then I am still a murderer," he said with a hollow voice. "There is still blood on me."

My anxious whisperings could not ease his guilt; he would wait for the sunrise.

Davie stayed close beside me all that evening and I began to realize how alone he had been for many days. We played silly little games with each other until bedtime.

My dreams that night were dark with fear. Fear for Robert, who blamed himself for the whole hunt, and especially fear for Tethani. I worried that I might have performed the burial preparations wrongly, that I might have forgotten something. I wondered again what his family had needed for the journey. I awoke several times, troubled with vague dreams of his family waiting for help, and me unable to give it. I could sense the answer just beyond my reach; I felt that if I thought hard enough, it would become clear.

Robert groaned several times in his sleep. Once he spoke, asking of the copper sunrise.

Davie slept quietly, content and innocent.

Towards morning, I became aware of a warm new feeling of peace flooding my body, reminding me of the happiness that brightened Tethani's face before he died, when he knew what more was needed. I lay still, letting the feeling flow over me, easing my tight muscles and soothing the clenched fibres of my being. My mind was free from sorrow and loneliness. I was at rest.

I imagined I heard the haunting notes of the copper flute; the beautiful magical music drifted through my brain, its sad rising and falling washing against my memory, sharpening my mind's images of Tethani during the happy times. That would be how he should be remembered.

The soft darkness surrounded me, but I knew Davie was awake beside me.

"Come with me, Davie," I said, and helped him sit up and dress. When we were dressed warmly, I took his hand and led him out the door into the cool night air.

Outside there was enough light to show the dim grey shapes of the village against the curtain of forest.

"Wait, Jamie," whispered Davie. He released my hand and slipped back beside the house. The still air chilled my fingers and suddenly I felt terribly alone, the way Tethani's family must have felt without him. I longed for Davie to come back, to be with me, but my feet would not move.

"Look, Jamie," said Davie, proudly holding the bead bracelet Tethani had once left for me. "It was on the ground, under the house. You can have it."

His hand pressed warmly back into mine, relieving my loneliness and bringing comfort.

I sensed then that Tethani's family had been waiting for a gift that only Tethani had been able to give, and I understood the smile on his lips. He was going with them to the West.

Davie and I walked together to the water.

For a long time we sat on the jetty, neither of us speaking, looking at the calm sea and the stars that broke through the wide openings in the clouds.

Davie pulled on his loose teeth and they came out in his hand. The empty space they left let his tongue slip out of place as he spoke. Once more I heard my name pronounced as "Tamie."

Off the end of the jetty a seal was splashing and barking happily, and Davie and I gazed at its games of chase.

Again I thought that I heard the music of Tethani's flute, and I looked up at the horizon.

All along the eastern sky the clouds were glowing brighter. It was a copper sunrise.